Papa Small

Random House 🏠 New York

For all the children who asked:
"Is there a Mama Small and Baby Small?"
Yes—Papa Small has a family.
Here they are—with my love.
Your friend,
Lois Lenski

Copyright © 1951 by Lois Lenski. Copyright renewed 1979 by Steven and Paul Covey.
All rights reserved under International and Pan-American Copyright Conventions. Published in
the United States by Random House Children's Books, a division of Random House, Inc.,
New York, and simultaneously in Canada by Random House of Canada Limited, Toronto.
Originally published by Henry Z. Walck, Inc., in 1951.

www.randomhouse.com/kids

Library of Congress Cataloging-in-Publication Data
Lenski, Lois.
Papa Small / Lois Lenski. — 1st Random House ed.
p. cm.
SUMMARY: After working, playing, and resting during the week, the congenial Small family goes
to church on Sunday and takes a ride in the car.
ISBN 0-375-82749-8 (trade) — ISBN 0-375-92749-2 (lib. bdg.)
[1. Family life—Fiction. 2. Week—Fiction.] I. Title.
PZ7.L54 Pap 2004
[E]—dc21
2003008113
MANUFACTURED IN MALAYSIA First Random House Edition 10 9 8 7 6 5 4 3 2 1
RANDOM HOUSE and colophon are registered trademarks of Random House, Inc.

PAPA SMALL

LOIS LENSKI

Random House New York

Papa Small has a family.
There is Mama Small and Baby Small.
There are the small Smalls,
Paul and Polly.
They live in a big house
on a hill.

Papa Small shaves
in the morning.
The small Smalls
like to watch.

Every morning
Papa Small goes away
to work.
Paul Small and Polly Small
wave good-bye.

Mama Small takes care
of the house.
She sweeps the floor.
The small Smalls help.

Mama Small cooks the meals.
Paul and Polly Small help.
They set the table.
Baby Small is hungry.

When Papa Small comes home,
the small Smalls
run to meet him.

Dinner is ready.
The Smalls sit down to eat.
Everything tastes good.

Mama Small washes the dishes.
Polly Small dries them.
Paul Small puts them away.
Papa Small rests.

On Monday
Mama Small washes the clothes.
When Papa Small comes home,
he helps hang them
on the line.

On Tuesday
Mama Small irons the clothes.
Papa Small puts on
a clean shirt.

Papa Small likes to help
around the house.
On Wednesday
he hangs a picture up
for Mama.

On Thursday
Papa Small fixes the kitchen sink.
The small Smalls watch.

On Friday
Papa Small cuts the grass.
Paul Small rakes it up.
Polly Small pushes Baby Small
in the buggy.
Mama Small rests.

On Saturday
the Smalls go to town.
Papa Small drives the little auto.
They come to the supermarket.
They park in front.

Papa and Mama Small buy groceries.

The small Smalls help.

Papa and Mama Small
and the small Smalls
take their groceries
to the little auto.
They drive home again.

Papa Small plows the garden.
Paul Small hoes.
Polly Small rakes.
Mama Small plants the seeds.

On Sunday
the Smalls go to church.
They drive in the little auto.
They park the car and walk.

The small Smalls sit still in church.
They listen and sing.
Papa Small sings, too.
Baby Small cries, and has to be
taken out.

When they get home,
Papa Small helps cook
Sunday dinner.
He brings in the food.

In the afternoon
the Smalls go out in the little auto.
They ride in the park.
The flowers are blooming.
The birds are singing.

When night comes,
the small Smalls are tired.
Papa Small reads them a story.
Mama Small gets the beds ready.

"Good night, Papa Small."
"Good night, Mama Small."

And
that's all
about
the small Smalls!